CATS'
NIGHT
OUT

For my book-loving friends,
Beth, Carrie, Julie, Laura, Susan,
and their many cats—C. S.

For Cleo—J. K.

SIMON & SCHUSTER BOOKS FOR YOUNG READERS
An imprint of Simon & Schuster Children's Publishing Division
1230 Avenue of the Americas, New York, New York 10020
Text copyright © 2010 by Caroline Stutson
Illustrations copyright © 2010 by J. Klassen
SIMON & SCHUSTER BOOKS FOR YOUNG READERS is a trademark of
Simon & Schuster, Inc.
Book design by Lucy Ruth Cummins
The text for this book is set in Old Times American.
The illustrations for this book are rendered digitally.
Manufactured in the United States of America 1210 PCR
10 9 8 7 6 5 4
Library of Congress Cataloging-in-Publication Data
Stutson, Caroline.
Cats' night out / Caroline Stutson ; illustrated by J. Klassen.—1st ed.
p. cm.
"A Paula Wiseman book."
Summary: Cats dance the night away out on the town, doing the tango, rumba, twist,
fox-trot, and more.
ISBN: 978-1-4169-4005-0 (hardcover)
[1. Stories in rhyme. 2. Cats—Fiction. 3. Dance—Fiction. 4. City and town life—Fiction.]
I. Klassen, J., ill. II. Title.
PZ8.3.S925Cat 2010
[E]—dc22
2008052268

CATS'
NIGHT
OUT

Caroline Stutson

Illustrated by J. Klassen

A Paula Wiseman Book
Simon & Schuster Books for Young Readers
New York London Toronto Sydney

From the alley, music drifts.
Shadows sway to a trumpet riff. . . .

Two cats samba, dressed in white,
on the rooftop Saturday night.

Four cats boogie, rock to blues,
in poodle skirts and saddle shoes.

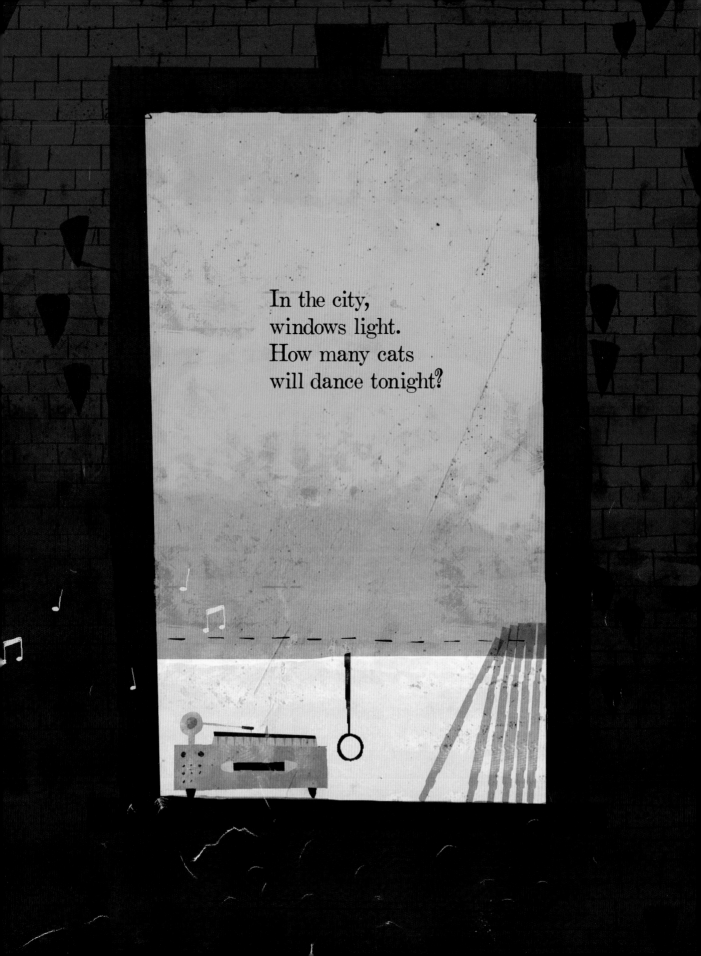

In the city,
windows light.
How many cats
will dance tonight?

Six cats tango in red capes

up and down the fire escapes.

Eight cats tap . . . tip bowler hats

in pink tuxedos, canvas spats.

8

Ten cats line-dance, keep the beat
in rhinestone boots on Easy Street.

Easy St

In the city,
windows light.
How many cats
will dance tonight?

Twelve town tabbies do the twist,

swinging their hips in dotted Swiss.

Fourteen fox-trot nose to nose,

dancing swiftly in evening clothes.

Sixteen rumba
in the dark,
twitching silk bottoms
through the park.

In the city,
windows light.
How many cats
will dance tonight?

Round and round,
they hop, skip, hop.

Twenty conga left and right

in splashy florals, plaids, and stripes.

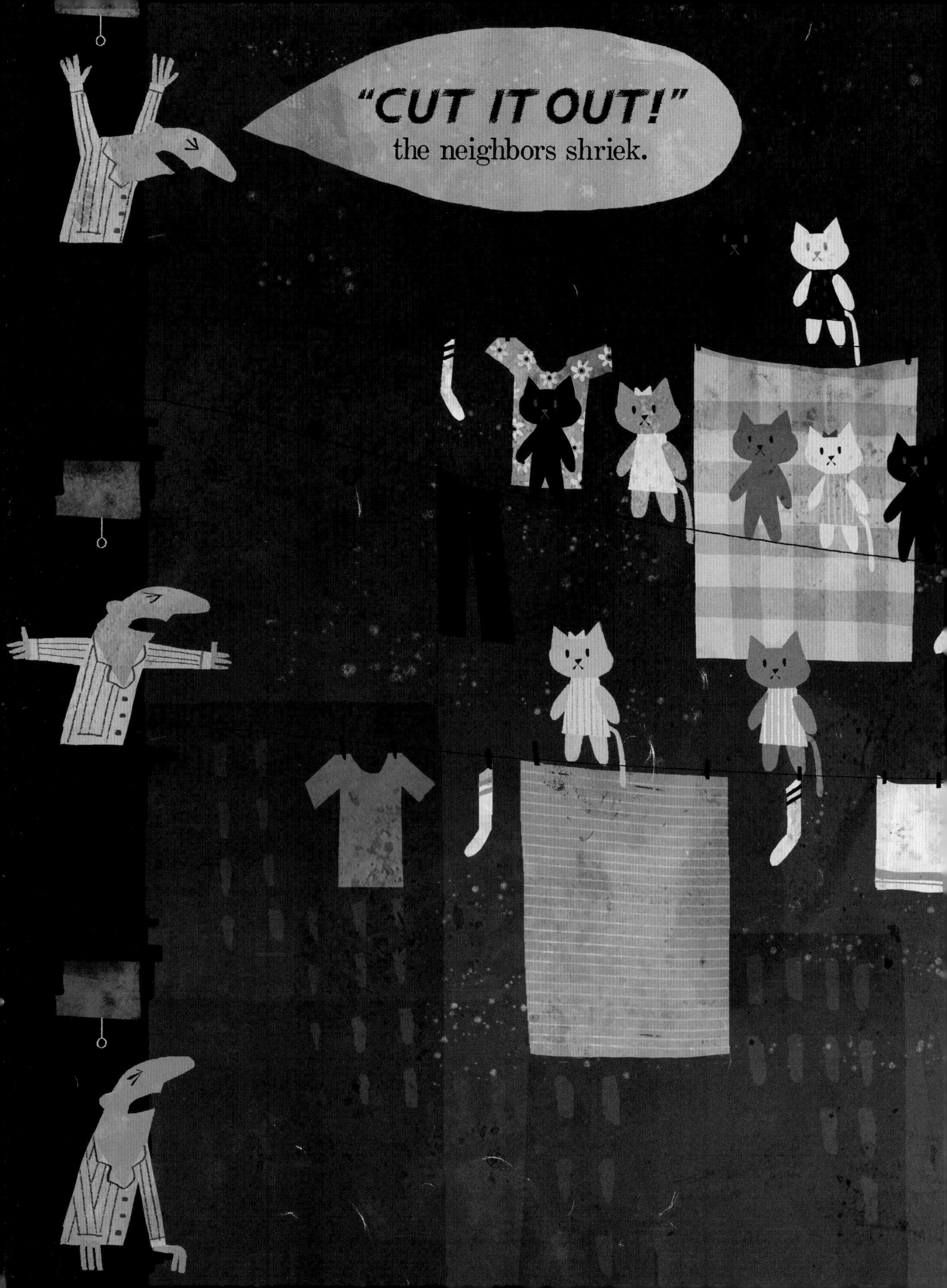
"CUT IT OUT!"
the neighbors shriek.

City cats slip off to sleep
while subways rumble,
taxis beep.

From the alley, music drifts.
Shadows sway to a trumpet riff.

Two cats waltz by neon light
n black half-masks on Sunday night. . . .